For William
~ J.S.
For Gorgeous George
~ J.C.

LITTLE TIGER PRESS
An imprint of Magi Publications
1 The Coda Centre, 189 Munster Road, London SW6 6AW
www.littletigerpress.com

First published in Great Britain 1998
by Little Tiger Press, London.
This edition published 2007

Text copyright © Julie Sykes 1998
Illustrations copyright © Jane Chapman 1998

ISBN 978-1-84506-690-1
Printed in China
2 4 6 8 10 9 7 5 3 1

Smudge

by
Julie Sykes
illustrated by
Jane Chapman

LITTLE TIGER PRESS

Smudge was playing in the backyard with his friends, Nibble the mouse and Bounce the rabbit. The sun was shining, and they were having so much fun that they didn't notice the big black cloud drifting overhead.

PLOP!

"What was that?" asked Smudge, looking up.

SPLASH! SPLATTER!

Suddenly the sky went dark, and large
raindrops began to fall.

"Watch out for the raindrops!" said Smudge.

"That one got me on the nose!"

"It's only a summer shower," said Nibble.

"It won't last."

"Help! We're getting wet!"
cried Smudge. "I'm going inside."
He raced toward the house,
but when he got there . . .

the door was shut!

"Let me in," barked Smudge. But no one heard him, even when he howled and scratched.

There must be another way inside, thought Smudge. Maybe the window's open.

The window *was* open—but it was too high for Smudge to reach. Under the window was a stack of flowerpots.

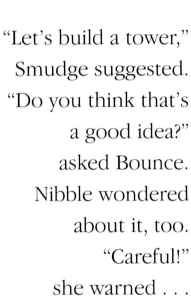

"Let's build a tower,"
Smudge suggested.
"Do you think that's
a good idea?"
asked Bounce.
Nibble wondered
about it, too.
"Careful!"
she warned . . .

CRASH!

It was too late! Smudge and the flowerpots tumbled to the ground.

"That didn't work," said Smudge, picking himself up. "But I have a better idea!"

"Oh no!" said Bounce.
"Not another one!"
"Let's go to your hutch,"
said Smudge. "It's dry in there."
Bounce led the way across
the backyard. Smudge followed
close behind.
"Wait for me!" cried Nibble.

"Come on, there's room for
everyone," Smudge said.
But . . .

there wasn't!

"What now?" asked Nibble.

"I know," said Smudge.

"Follow me, everyone. I've got an even better idea!"

Nibble and Bounce followed Smudge back to the house. Smudge got there first.

"What's next?" said Bounce. "I'm almost afraid to ask."

"It's easy," said Smudge, as he poked his nose through the cat door.

And it *was* easy until . . .

he got stuck!

"I knew it!" said Bounce.

"What am I supposed to do now?" cried Smudge.

"Stop wriggling and we'll give you a paw," said Nibble.

So Nibble and Bounce pushed Smudge as hard as they could. They pushed and pushed and

PUSHED

until . . .

POP!
Smudge shot
through the
cat door
and landed,
nose first,
on the mat.

"That was easy!" he cried,
shaking himself dry.

"Come along, Nibble,
it's your turn next,"
he said. But when
Smudge looked
outside through
the cat door
he saw . . .

that the rain had stopped!
It was only a shower after all.
Nibble and Bounce were playing
together in the backyard, and, once
again, the sun was shining.
"Wait!" cried Smudge. "I want to play, too,
but . . .

how am I going to get out again?"

Smudge looked around. . . .

Then he had a *great* idea. . . .